First published in 1996 by Sapling,
an imprint of Boxtree Ltd, Broadwall House,
21 Broadwall, London SE1 9PL
Copyright © Geoffrey Planer, 1996

10 9 8 7 6 5 4 3 2 1

Except for use in a review, no part of this book
may be reproduced, stored in a retrieval system
or transmitted in any form or by any means,
electronic, mechanical, photocopying, recording or
otherwise, without prior permission of the publisher.

Reproduction by SX Composing DTP
Printed and bound in Great Britain by Cambus Litho Ltd.

ISBN: 0 7522 2355 0

A CIP catalogue entry for this book
is available from the British Library.

# The Polar Bear who Lost his Name

Geoffrey Planer

sapling

For Erica
(who always has her
feet on the ground)

*'Please, please, pretty please –*
*it's too daytimey to go to bed.'*
*'It is way, way past bedtime*
*already,' said Mrs Tail firmly.*
*'But it's all sunny still; with*
*blue sky and clouds,' said Julia.*
*She peeped out of the window.*
*'I wish I could go and live*
*on the clouds,' she added.*
*'I knew someone who knew*
*someone who went there once,' said*
*Mrs Tail, drawing the curtains quickly.*
*Mrs Tail sat down on the bed*
*and opened the book.*

*Another Night,*
*Another Mouse,*
*Another Tale . . .*

# The Polar Bear who Lost his Name

Tom Happyapple never wanted to go to sleep. But sometimes he did quite like going to bed, because sometimes (and he could never tell quite when it would happen) he could get his bed to fly.

Each night he would feel down the side of his bed, the side next to the wall where the sheet was cool, to see if his Control Panel had appeared. If it had, he would press the buttons, the bedroom curtains would draw back, the windows would open and he and his friend Sergeant (the monkey who sat on his bed) would fly out into the night.

He never took Pippin, his younger sister, with him because she was always asleep. One evening in the middle of summer, when it just wouldn't get dark, Tom's luck was in. He found the Control Panel down in the usual place. He pushed the buttons; the engine under the bed started, the curtains opened, the windows too, and Tom and Sergeant held on tight.

They were about to take off when Tom saw that Pippin was awake. 'Want to come too?' he asked, rather hoping that she wouldn't. Pippin was wide eyed; she nodded and quickly jumped onto Tom's bed.

Just in time too, for the bed lifted silently off from the floor and flew straight out of the open windows and into the evening sky. Pippin couldn't believe what was happening and she clung on tight to the sheets. Tom had been on quite a few flights and so he was used to it all and good at steering now.

'Where would you like to go?' he asked her. 'We can go and see cowboys or we can go to Brazil ...

or we can go and track monster dinosaurs.' Pippin shook her head. 'Can we go up in the clouds and see if there are fairies there?' she asked.

'Huh. S'pose so,' said Tom pulling a face. Sergeant pulled a face too, but since it was Pippin's treat, Tom (quite nicely) made the bed shoot straight up into the night clouds.

They pulled the sheets right up around them and held on extra tightly. A cold wind whistled through their hair – it was really exciting. They went high, high up into the clouds. It got colder. Tom landed the bed as gently as he could on a huge white one.

Rather slyly he let Pippin get out first
to see if it was hard enough to walk on –
or whether you fell straight through.
'Like walking on fluffy bits,' she said
delightedly. She tried jumping.
It was like a bouncy castle.
'Like bouncy fluffy bits,' she said.

Tom and Sergeant jumped down and started to bounce too. It was better than a bouncy castle, but icy on their feet.

'Where are the fairies?' asked Pippin. 'Don't be silly; no one lives up here,' said Tom.

At that minute they saw something
move behind one of the clouds.

It was a white polar bear. They decided
they should climb back onto the bed
rather quickly and take off,
but before they could ...

... they saw it was a small polar bear, looking rather sad. It was coming towards them.

'It's a baby polo bear,' said Tom. 'What's your name polo bear?' he asked as it came closer.

'I don't know, I've lost it,' said the polar bear sadly. 'I've been looking for it everywhere; the others won't let me play with them if I haven't got a name.'

'Others?' asked Pippin, shivering.

'Yes – the other polar bears. We live here; with the fairies.'

Tom and Sergeant looked at each other.
'We could help you find a name,' said Tom.
'How about Alfred?' he suggested.
The little bear shook its head.

'How about Justin?
Hugo? or Tom?'
The bear shook
its head again.

'William? Simon?
or Richard?'
The little bear
shook its head
some more.

'You're not a girl, are you?'
asked Tom suspiciously.
The bear shook its head again.

'How 'bout just polo brrrrrrr,'
said Pippin, whose teeth were
chattering with cold now.

The polar bear
looked up.
'That's it!'
it said.

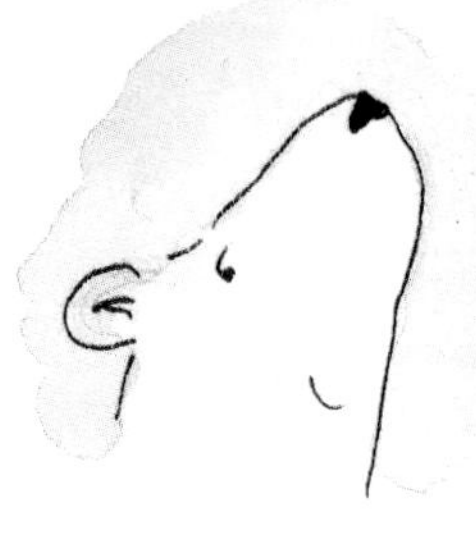

'What is?' asked
Tom and Pippin
and Sergeant.

'That's my name!'
said the polar bear
delightedly.

'You found my name –
I'm a Polobrrr! Oh
you are clever!'

'It just sort of jumped out of my mouth 'cause I was cold,' said Pippin, very pleased to have helped.

The polar bear
was delighted.
It danced
around on
its back legs
singing,
'My name's
Polobrrr.
My name's
Polobrrr.
I'm a Polobrrr ...'
It started
to run off,
but stopped –
remembering
its manners

It scampered back to Tom, Pippin
and Sergeant on the bed.
'Thank you very much for finding my
name,' it said. 'Will you come back to
see us one day?' asked the Polobrrr.

Pippin nodded her head.

'And the fairies?' it added.

'Oh yes,' she said nodding
her head even harder.

Tom and Sergeant just
looked at each other.

*'Well, that's a bit of a daft story isn't it?' said Mrs Tail, closing the book. 'Though I quite like it myself in a way,' she added. 'Anyway, it's a bit darker now,' she said, looking out of the window. ' So you shouldn't have too much trouble getting to sleep.'*

*She turned around and looked down. Julia was fast asleep. Mrs Tail smiled.*

*'Talking to myself, as usual.'*

*'Sleep Tight for all Tails,' said Mrs Tail.*

*She tiptoed out of the room and went round the house to make sure that the 364 other mice were also sound asleep.*

*Small Tales,*
*Tall Tales,*
*Bedtime -*
*for All Tails*